For Thomas and Maddie, with love ~ M C B
To Noah, Levi and Isaac ~ J C

Copyright © 2008 by Good Books, Intercourse, PA 17534
International Standard Book Number: 978-1-56148-610-6

Library of Congress Catalog Card Number: 2007031720

Text copyright © M. Christina Butler 2008
Illustrations copyright © Jane Chapman 2008
Original edition published in English by Little Tiger Press,
an imprint of Magi Publications, London, England, 2008.
Printed in Singapore

Library of Congress Cataloging-in-Publication Data
Butler, M. Christina.
The dark, dark night / M. Christina Butler ; [illustrated by] Jane Chapman.
p. cm.
Summary: Upon awakening from his long winter's nap, Frog spends a
happy day playing with his friends but when he reaches his pond after dark,
he sees a huge pond monster and needs his friends' help to face it.
ISBN 978-1-56148-610-6 (alk. paper)
[1. Night--Fiction. 2. Fear of the dark--Fiction.
3. Shadows--Fiction. 4. Animals--Fiction. 5. Ponds--Fiction.]
I. Chapman, Jane, 1970– ill. II. Title.

PZ7.B97738Dar 2008
[E]--dc22
2007031720

The Dark, Dark Night

M. Christina Butler   Jane Chapman

Good Books

Intercourse, PA 17534
800/762-7171
www.GoodBooks.com

Frog was very excited. All winter he had been asleep under a stone, and now that it was spring, he was on his way back to his pond.

On the way, he bumped into
Badger and Hedgehog.

Then he played leapfrog with
Rabbit and Mouse.

Suddenly, he saw that it was getting dark,
so he borrowed a lantern from Mouse and
off he went through the woods to the pond.
   Woo-woo! the wind blew in the trees.
   Squeak-squeak! went the lantern, as it
swung from side to side.
   And the dark was all around.

When Frog reached his home, he put the
lantern down behind him and was just about
to jump into the water, when he saw . . .

. . . a huge, black Pond Monster,
with enormous claws, coming
out of the reeds!

Frog grabbed the lantern and hopped as
fast as he could back through the woods.

"There's a huge monster in the pond!" he cried.
  "Are you sure?" laughed Hedgehog.
  Frog nodded, trembling.
  "All right," said Hedgehog, calmly. "We'll
have a look together."
  "And I'll come too," said Mouse.

Off they went through the woods.
    Woo-woo! the wind blew in the trees.
    Squeak-squeak! went the lanterns.
    "Wait for me!" cried Mouse.
    And the dark was all around.

Soon Hedgehog and Frog reached the pond.
    "Now," said Hedgehog, "where's this
monster . . . ?"

"There it is!" cried Frog.

It was bigger than before, with enormous claws and terrible spikes down its back!

"Run! Run!" cried Hedgehog. "Pond Monster! Pond Monster!"

"What's all this?" chuckled Rabbit. "A monster?
There's no such thing as monsters!"

"Come and see for yourself," said Hedgehog,
shivering.

"All right," said Rabbit. "I will."

"I'll never swim in my pond again!"
sniffed Frog as they set off through
the woods.

Woo-woo! blew the wind in the trees.
Squeak-squeak! went the lanterns.
"Wait for me!" cried Mouse.
And the dark was all around.

It wasn't long before they were back at the pond.
Rabbit, Hedgehog and Frog tiptoed to the water.
   There it was again, the big Pond Monster.
It was bigger than ever!
   It had enormous claws, terrible spikes down
its back, two big horns and wildly waving arms!

"Run for your life!" yelled Rabbit, racing back through the woods, with Hedgehog and Frog close behind.

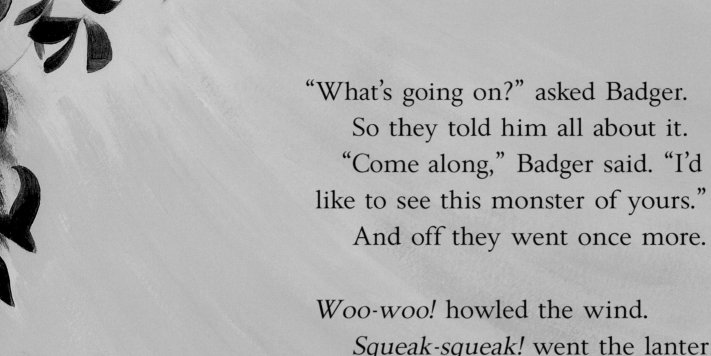

"What's going on?" asked Badger.
So they told him all about it.
"Come along," Badger said. "I'd
like to see this monster of yours."
And off they went once more.

Woo-woo! howled the wind.
Squeak-squeak! went the lanterns.
"Wait for me!" cried Mouse.
And the dark was all around.

As they reached the pond, a huge gust of
wind came through the trees and blew out
all the lanterns!

"I can't see a monster," said Badger at last.
   "That's because it's too dark,"
whispered Frog.
   And there they all stood, waiting in
the moonlight for something to happen.

Just then, Mouse caught up with
the others, at last.

"Yooo-hooo!" she shouted, waving
from the bank.

Badger, Rabbit, Hedgehog and Frog
looked at Mouse. And then they
looked at the small, black shape
waving from the reeds.

"Look at that!" said Hedgehog.

"That's not a Pond Monster," said Rabbit.

"That's Mouse's shadow!" said Frog.

"I can't believe it!" said Badger. "You were running from your shadows every time!"

The four friends laughed and laughed and laughed. "Hurray!" cried Frog. "There's no monster after all!" And with a huge, happy

SPLASH!

he leaped into his lovely pond—at last.